There's a
Sea Witch in
My Swim Class

Written by **Sam Hay**

Illustrated by **Ria Maria Lee**

Disney • **Hyperion**

Los Angeles   New York

First Hardcover Edition, June 2023
First Paperback Edition, June 2023
10 9 8 7 6 5 4 3 2 1
FAC-004510-23118
Printed in the United States of America

This book is set in Aptifer Slab LT Pro/Linotype
Designed by Zareen Johnson
Illustrations created in Photoshop
Stock images: frame 1721120479, sign 1723931281/Shutterstock

Library of Congress Cataloging-in-Publication Data

Names: Hay, Sam, author.
Title: There's a sea witch in my swim class / Sam Hay.
Description: First edition. • Los Angeles ; New York : Disney-Hyperion, 2023. • Series: Camp Lil' Vills ; Book 3 • Audience: Ages 6–8 • Audience: Grades 1–3 • Summary: "Ursula makes a splash at Camp Lilliputian Villains when Bloom and her friends head to Lake Whisper"— Provided by publisher.
Identifiers: LCCN 2021970064 (print) • LCCN 2021970114 (ebook) • ISBN 9781368084628 (hardcover) • ISBN 9781368057417 (paperback) • ISBN 9781368074094 (ebk)
Subjects: CYAC: Magic—Fiction. • Camps—Fiction. • Animals, Mythical—Fiction. • Lake animals—Fiction. • LCGFT: Animal fiction. • Humorous fiction.
Classification: LCC PZ7.H31387385 Th 2023 (print) • LCC PZ7.H31387385 (ebook) • DDC [Fic]—dc23
LC record available at https://lccn.loc.gov/2021970064
LC ebook record available at https://lccn.loc.gov/2021970114

Visit www.DisneyBooks.com

CALLING ALL LILLIPUTIAN CAMPERS!

If you're feeling hotter than a husky on a beach vacation, why not cool down by Lake Whisper and discover all the magical aquatic activities?

· Fly through the air on a winged dolphin!

· Try stargazing with a snorkel in Big Skies Bay!

· Marvel at the mysteries of the lake on a midnight underwater safari!

· Gallop through the surf on a giant sea horse!

· And look out for our legendary wish fish!

Don't forget to book your place at the sunset BBQ at Sparkle Lagoon.*

*SEE PERIWINKLE FOR DETAILS.

SPARKLE LAGOON

FLYING CANOE DOCK

THE SHAKE SHIP

BIG SKIES BAY

Lake Whisper

1

I closed my eyes and twisted the strings of my enchanted friendship bracelet and made my wish. *Please make me disappear so I don't have to join swim class.*

"Hey, Bloom! Look at me!" I opened my eyes, and saw my buddy Benji's head pop up out of the water below the big rock I was sitting on.

Aw, pickled potions! I groaned. Not that I'd expected the spell to work. Enchanted friendship bracelets were useful if you wanted to change the color of your nails or turn your hands into bunny paws, but they didn't have enough magic to make you vanish.

"Check out my frogs' legs spell," Benji yelled, poking his webbed toes out of the water. "See how great they look. . . . They're *toad-ally* awesome!" He suddenly sneezed, the spell triggering his magical allergies.

I let out a small smile. "Yeah, they're amazing. And they're really making you swim well."

He beamed up at me, and I noticed his magic glasses had turned into multicolored goggles. "So, when are you coming in to try some water magic?"

"Er, in a moment," I said, pretending to fiddle with my bracelet. "I don't want this to slip off."

Benji and I had made the friendship bracelets the day before at Crafty Corner. I'd threaded a thick enchanted cotton through the middle of mine—sparkle silver for strength.

"Ooh, Bloom, look, there's an extra deep spot!" Benji called. "If we're very lucky we might spot the kraken."

I gulped.

"Imagine . . ." Benji had a dreamy look on his face. "If the kraken actually appeared right now, we'd get to swim with it!"

My heart started to race at the thought. *More like become its afternoon snack!*

"Oh, look at the time," Benji said, as a clock appeared on the frames of his magical goggles. "It's almost two o'clock! We've got the charmed rock-skipping class in ten minutes."

I nodded, but inside I felt wobblier than a giant bowl of jumping jelly. *If only Benji hadn't got so excited about the lake,* I thought as I shuffled a little closer to the edge of the rock and tried to summon up the courage to dive in.

Normally, Benji's high energy and enthusiasm about everything at camp was great. But that was before he'd learned about Lake Whisper....

After three super sunny days that were hotter than a cauldron on fast-boil mode, Benji couldn't wait to get in the water to cool off. And as soon as we arrived and he heard about the camp water activities, he immediately wanted to try them all. So far today we'd already been wand surfing, water wheeling, and dragon-boat racing. He'd zipped from the shallow shore to the deeper middle and everything in between, pointing out all the watery creatures and features he spotted. Benji had even insisted we eat our picnic lunch perched on a floating platform in the pelican petting zone!

"Is it true that the rocks change when you stand on them?" Benji asked, kicking his flippers. "Because one of my bunkmates said he saw one turn into a real live unicorn-shark! Cool, huh?"

"Uh, yeah." I peered over the edge of the boulder into the swirling blue and shivered.

When Dad had first opened the Lilliputian Villages Summer Camp in the middle of a magical forest, I couldn't wait to get involved. I loved helping out with the campers and organizing the activities. . . . But the lake was my least favorite spot. The thought of going underwater made me sweatier than a squid stuck in quicksand.

Water magic was just too unpredictable. I hated feeling so out of my depth. Spells never worked like they're supposed to. Besides, most of the activities on the lake sounded terrifying: levitation hover-boarding, flying-dolphin riding. Underwater gardening! And when one of the counselors let slip about the kraken, it just made me even more determined to stay on dry land. So far, my avoidance plan had mostly worked. Until now. . . .

I watched Benji splash past my boulder again with the other campers in the swimming-spell class. I didn't want to let him down. But what if the weird currents washed me away? Or I got grabbed by the water trolls? Or jabbed by a sword shrimp? Or . . . or . . . or I just couldn't hold my breath long enough! I shuddered. *Calm down*, I told myself, *maybe you can convince Benji to go do one of the beachside activities instead, like sand-shaping spells or crab-charming. . . .*

Just then I heard a cry.

"Hey!" I called, waving to a mer-kid sobbing in the shallows. "Are you okay?"

She gave a little sniff and pointed underwater. "That plant just stole my bubble ball!"

I grimaced. A grabby-branched bramble bush, no doubt. They were really mean water weeds—sharp and spiky—that liked to reach out and take your belongings just for the fun of it. The only thing that worked on them was a tickle-release spell.

"It's okay," I called to the mer-kid as tiny, pearly tears streaked down her cheeks. "I'll—um—see if I can get your bubble ball back." I glanced nervously into the water. *Come on, Bloom, you have to help.* I took a deep breath and counted to three. . . . Then I pushed off the rock and slipped into the water, keeping my head well above the surface. *Broomsticks crossed, nothing gets me!*

I doggy-paddled about, trying to remember the words of the tickle spell. Dad had taught it to me when one of his greedy houseplants had tried to eat my dog.

But as I swam closer, I felt a powerful swell of water sweep me out of the way. A purple-colored head popped up in front, heading straight for the mer-girl.

"Relax!" I heard the purple-headed kid say in a smooth, silky voice that sounded a lot more grown-up than she looked. "I'm Ursula. I'm a sea witch in training, and I've got a potion to make that oversize seedling let go of your bubble." She revealed a bulging belt bag tied around her middle, which she flipped open and began rooting around inside.

"Ah, yes," she purred, plucking out a small

brown bottle. "This should do the trick. I'll have your ball back in seconds—" She paused for a moment, looking at the young mer-girl's hair. "Ooh, I love your golden headband. It's so sparkly and shiny. If only I had one like that..." She sighed. "It would just be soooo nice to be gifted one."

Huh? I blinked the water out of my eyes. *Did I hear right? It sounds like she wants the mer-girl to give her the headband!* I tipped my head from side-to-side, in case I'd got pondweed in my ears. *Nobody would expect to be paid by a little kid who'd lost their ball. . . . Would they?*

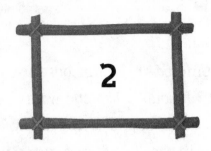

2

URSULA disappeared underwater, flicking her long purple tentacles out behind her. Then she burst back up, clutching the mer-kid's bubble ball in her hands. "Ha! That pesky plant won't be taking any more trinkets for a while." She tossed the ball to the little girl and glided forward, her tentacles reaching toward the crown of her head.

"Hey!" I gasped. "You're not going to take her headband, are you?"

But the girl had already handed it over, and Ursula quickly shoved it into a shell-shaped purse. "Headband?" she said, peering at me with a confused expression on her face. "What headband?"

"The one she was wearing..." I said, turning to look at the mer-kid, then finding she had vanished underwater.

"Bloom! Bloom!" Just then, Benji came splashing across the lake, his magic goggles fogged up. "Something amazing just happened."

"It did?"

"Yeah, I just managed to get us in the giant sea horse–surfing class starting in five minutes."

"B-b-but what about the rock skipping?" I stammered. At least rock skipping was ABOVE the lake. Sea horse surfing—I gulped—usually involved going underwater.

Benji smiled. "Don't worry. I've rescheduled. Now we can do *both*!"

"Oh—yeah, that's great, I guess."

Ursula coughed. "Pardon me, angelfish," she said, smiling at me. "You look a little"—she paused and cocked her head to one side as though she was studying my face—"*shell-shocked*. Don't you like sea horses?"

I felt my cheeks burn. "No, no, I like sea horses. It's just that . . . well . . . last time I tried it, my sea horse kind of got a little overexcited and it threw me off. I sank pretty deep and—"

"Oh, Bloom! I'm so sorry." Benji's smile vanished. "We don't have to."

"No, no, it's fine. I'm happy to give it another try." Though I wished I didn't have to do it *right now*.

Ursula nodded as if she could hear my thoughts. "You know, I've got *just* the thing." She flipped open the bag on her belt and rummaged inside. "Yes, here it is—Saddle Glue!" She held up a small red bottle. "Guaranteed to make you stick to your seat!"

"Oh, that looks shiny," Benji said.

"And so does that!" Ursula said, peering at my friendship bracelet.

Huh? Is she angling for a trade with me *now?* "Uh—no thanks," I said, covering my bracelet with my other hand.

"Suit yourself!" Ursula dropped the bottle back into her bag, and her shoulders slumped a little.

I felt a twinge of guilt. *Maybe she was just trying to help and I judged her too fast. Dad's always telling me to give people a chance.* "Um—it was really kind of you to offer, though."

But Ursula didn't hear me. "Oh, dear," she murmured, peering over my shoulder. "That boy seems to have lost his watch." In a blink, she was gone.

"Are you sure you want to try sea horse surfing?" Benji asked. "Because if you'd rather not—"

"No, it's fine," I said. "I mean, what's the worst that could happen?" *That you fall off, sink underwater, and get swallowed up by the kraken perhaps?* I grimaced. *Stop it, Bloom,* I told myself. *No camper has ever been eaten by a sea monster.*

At least, not that I know of.

3

"**UM—BLOOM**, can you tell me that spell again?" Benji whispered as we led our sea horses out into the deeper waters of the lake.

"You mean the float-like-a-boat spell?"

It was part of our safety lesson by Jordy, the merman counselor. If you fell off your sea horse, you just had to say the magic words and you'd bob straight back up to the surface. At least that's what Jordy *said* would happen. I was hoping not to have to test it out!

"Sure . . . it's *'Flotsam, Jetsam, make me float! Straight to the surface like a boat!'* But don't forget Jordy said you also have to put your hands together above your head and blow through your nose, or it won't work."

"Thanks!" Benji stroked his sea horse's neck. It whinnied, and sparkly bubbles popped out of its nostrils. "Aw, I love sea horses. Are you excited, Bloom?"

Excited wasn't the word I'd use. Terrified, maybe. Petrified, definitely. Panicked, absolutely! I patted my sea horse with a shaky hand, then put my foot into the stirrup. *Okay, here goes nothing.* But as I pulled myself into the saddle, expecting my sea horse to take off like last time, I was surprised to feel it stop and hover in the water until I was settled. *Huh? This actually feels okay.*

"Don't worry, Bloom," Jordy called to me as he swam past. "Barra is the gentlest sea horse. She'll look after you."

I nodded and patted her neck.

"Come on, Bloom," Benji called. "Let's head into the waves."

I gripped the reins and shrank deeper into the saddle, preparing myself in case Barra decided she wasn't feeling so gentle after all. But she bobbed smoothly across the water.

"Isn't this awesome!" Benji called from ahead. "This might be my favorite activity yet—Ooh, look...is that a hover paddleboard class over there? I can't wait to try that!"

But I didn't reply. I'd noticed a small group of campers treading water nearby. Right in the middle was—

"Ursula!" *Hey, did she just take that little sprite's cap?*

"Watch out, Bloom, big—" But Benji's warning was lost in the noise of the crashing wave that came from nowhere.

"Whoa!" Suddenly I was falling, then plunging underwater, where a strange current swept me into a spin. I held my breath, puffing out my cheeks, trying to fight against the whirling tide. *Quick, Bloom,* I told myself. *Use the float-like-a-boat spell.* But the waves were making me dizzy, and the words kept getting muddled in my mind.

Just then, a dark shape swept toward me....

Huh? Is it the kraken?

But it wasn't the sea monster. A familiar silky voice sounded in my ear: "I'll help you get back to the surface. I just need your bracelet!"

Ursula? I blinked through the watery blur. It was hard to tell who or what was bobbing alongside me.

"Give me the bracelet," the voice sounded again.

4

I peered through the watery gloom, my eyes wide, my cheeks feeling like they were about to burst. But before I could think of how to reply, I felt a gentle nudge on my arm. . . .

Barra?

The sea horse was pushing me away from the swirling current, and suddenly the words of the floating spell seemed to settle in my mind.

Flotsam, Jetsam, make me float,
Straight to the surface like a boat.

I put my hands above my head and blew through my nose. Instantly I bobbed back to the surface, spluttering and coughing and trying to catch my breath.

"*ACHOO!* Bloom! Are you okay?" Benji zoomed over on his sea horse, his face pale, the frames of his goggles flashing red. He sneezed again, then—"Did you just do the float-like-a-boat spell?" he asked, wiping his nose with the back of his hand. "Because my magical allergies have gone into overdrive!"

I nodded, still too breathless to reply. Instead, I wrapped my arms around Barra's neck and hugged her. "Thank you," I whispered when I could.

Then I turned back to Benji. "Hey, did you see Ursula just now? I thought I heard her asking about my bracelet and—"

"Hmmm... isn't that her over there?" Benji pointed to the far side of the lake.

I looked where he was looking. *Huh? How could she be in two places at once?* "That's weird. I guess the strange water magic just made me think I saw her nearby." I shuddered. I'd definitely had enough of the lake. "How about a snack break?"

Benji's eyes lit up. "Yes, please! Let's swim over to the Shake Ship. I've heard they do awesome ice cream seashells."

Oof. The Shake Ship was a snack shack in the very center of the lake.

Benji dismounted from his sea horse and started waving good-bye.

"Come on, Bloom!" he said, doing a tumble turn in the direction of the floating snack bar.

"Bye, Barra," I said, letting go of the sea horse's neck. "And thank you again."

I followed Benji, carefully keeping my head above the surface until the shack came into view. The Shake Ship consisted of a wooden snack shack surrounded by several jetties with different seating areas. Most were halfway under the lake, so the water-dwelling campers could use them. As I got closer, I saw the place was packed with mer-kids, sea sprites, pond gnomes, and a group of giggly-looking swamp fairies. . . .

"Hey, Bloom!" Benji smiled as I pulled myself up onto the jetty next to him. "Don't worry. I'll get the ice cream for us. You look pooped."

He wasn't wrong. He headed off, and I lay back on the warm wooden jetty, enjoying the feeling of being on dry land for a moment, even if it was swaying slightly.

But then I heard a familiar voice....

"Oh, what a *marvelous* box! I've *always* wanted one like that."

Ursula? I looked across to one of the seating areas. The young sea witch was sitting with a swamp fairy.

23

"I think I've changed my mind," the fairy said, ruffling her webbed wings. "I'm not sure I want the potion now."

"No returns!" Ursula folded her arms.

"Um—hello—is everything okay here?" I asked as I headed over.

Ursula glanced up at me. "Ooh, everything's just *fin-tastic*, thank you."

The swamp fairy gave a sad little sniffle, then pushed a small shell box across the sunken table, and fluttered off into the water.

"Wait—" I called. "Are you okay?" But she'd already gone. I looked at Ursula, who was stuffing the box in her purse. "Did you take that from her?"

"*Take* it? Of course not!" Ursula cocked her head to one side. "It was a gift! She asked for a singing potion for talent night, and in return she wanted me to have her jewelry box. So *kind* of her."

"But I thought I heard her say she'd changed her mind."

Ursula made a shocked face. "Oh, Bloom, you must have misheard. She was just so grateful for my help. Between you and me"—she leaned in closer—"the poor thing sings like a swamp frog. She was terrified of making a fool of herself. That's when I stepped in. I *live* to help others."

I frowned. Had I heard wrong? My ears did still feel a little blocked after being under the water. I was about to apologize when there was a sudden *SPLASH*, and an enormous dark shape shot out of the lake and leaped over our heads, momentarily blocking the light.

"Argh!" Ursula gasped.

"Walloping wands!" Benji cried, spilling the ice cream he was carrying over. "What was that thing?"

But I knew exactly what it was.

5

"**DAD!**" I breathed as the dolphin resurfaced, changing back into human form. He stepped onto the jetty, then shook out his cloak and strode toward us. Every head turned to look. I puffed out my chest with pride. No one could do magical transformations like my dad.

"Whoa, Mr. Maj," Benji breathed. "That was awesome!"

Dad chuckled. "Well, there's nothing quite like a refreshing dip to cool off on a hot afternoon. Don't you agree, Benji?"

"Um—sure." Benji pushed his goggles up his nose, leaving sticky ice cream smudges on the frames.

"Bloom, I hope you're having a fine day." Dad smiled at me, then turned to Ursula. "Hello there. What's your name?"

"I'm Ursula."

"Of course." Dad bowed to her. "A talented sea witch, if I'm not mistaken."

"Well, I don't like to *fish* for compliments," she said with a smirk, "but you're not wrong."

"Indeed," Dad said. "I was actually hoping you'd all use your gifts to help me with something." He took a seat on the sunken picnic bench next to us, and I noticed his clothes were dry as a bone. *So magical!* I thought proudly.

"I'm looking for volunteers to assist with

'Enchanted Splash Time' this afternoon," Dad went on. "It's a class for younger campers," he added in case Benji and Ursula hadn't heard of it. "For some of our visitors, it is their first introduction to the joys of water magic."

I felt a wave of relief. I loved helping with the little ones. And anything that took me away from the deep waters of the lake sounded perfect. "I'll do it," I said. "It's in Sparkle Lagoon, right?"

Dad nodded.

"Ooh, I've read about Sparkle Lagoon," Benji said, the frames of his goggles glowing. "Are there really sea turtles you can ride on? And golden flamingos that you can groom? And real wish fish?"

"Well, the fish are quite rare," Dad said. "But they do grant temporary wishes."

Benji's eyes widened. "I definitely want to see one of those."

"And what about you, Ursula?" Dad said. "Would you like to lend a hand?"

Ursula shrugged. "Of course. I'm *always*

happy to be a community fish and help others. Right, Bloom?"

"Oh, um—yeah," I mumbled. *Though you do seem to enjoy getting things in return!*

Dad looked at me and raised an eyebrow. I blushed. *Oops, why do I always forget he can read minds!* As a reformed evil sorcerer Dad always tried to see the best in people, and he never liked anyone to be misjudged.

"Thank you all," Dad said. "Volunteering is so rewarding. I think we sometimes underestimate people. But when we spend quality time together, we can see what they're really capable of."

I nodded. It was so true. When I first met Benji I thought he was a little clumsy and silly. But he turned out to be the kindest, most helpful friend ever. *Maybe I need to give Ursula a chance to show us what a lovely person she is, too.*

Dad smiled. "I shall tell Periwinkle to expect you."

"Oh, Periwinkle is the best," I said. Although

I didn't take part in most lake activities, I often joined the beachside picnics, and Periwinkle was one of the most energetic water-based counselors.

Dad stood up. "And now I must fly." He clapped his hands together.

"There he goes!" Benji cried as a large black dragonfly darted across our heads and over the lake. "Your dad is so cool."

And wise, too. I glanced at Ursula. Maybe helping little kids—for *free*—would show Ursula that you don't always need something in return, gift or not. *Broomsticks crossed!*

"So, where's this Sparkle Lagoon?" Ursula asked.

"It's at the other end of the lake," I said. "Just past the Flying Canoe dock . . ."

"All right, well . . ." Ursula slipped into the lake. "Last one to the lagoon is a *dreadfully* slow sea snail!"

"Come on, Bloom!" Benji called. "We don't want to be a sea snail."

Um—I don't mind being a sea snail! I glanced around. "Wait—maybe we could hitch a ride?" I pointed to the rainbow ride-a-swans gathered on the other side of the jetty. The swans were real boat-shaped birds that floated up and down the lake, giving weary campers a rest. "They're friendly," I called to Benji. "And always travel *above* water!"

But he had already dived into the lake and was swimming frantically after Ursula.

Phantoms' pants! I muttered. *Why does everyone love the water so much?* I glanced into the swirly blue-green waves and tried to summon up the courage to follow them.

Nah! I'll take the swan, thank you very much.

6

BY the time I reached the other end of the lake on my bird boat, Ursula and Benji were sitting waiting on a large rock outside Sparkle Lagoon.

"Bloom!" Benji dived off to meet me. Ursula followed, smirking at my swan.

"Oh, Bloom, you really should let me help you with your fear of water," she said. "I have the *perfect* potion to fix it."

"I'm not scared," I muttered, clambering off the bird. "I—um—just like swans."

"Of course. Whatever floats your boat," Ursula said.

But as soon as I began to wade into the lagoon, my crankiness evaporated. Tiny neon fish darted past my legs. Shimmering shells glistened in the sand around my toes. And I could hear the musical coral singing softly. I sighed. There was something about the peaceful shallow lagoon that instantly made you feel calmer.

"Hey, is that a golden flamingo?" Benji asked.

"Yep," I said, as the long-legged bird strutted past us. "It's probably heading over for groom time. Golden flamingos love a bit of pampering."

"Oh, I can't wait to try that." Benji smiled. "But first I want to see a wish fish."

"I could find one for you," Ursula said. "I have a potion that can find anything. You just say the magic words."

"That's not really the spirit of wish-fish spotting," I said. "They're special because not many people see them."

Ursula snorted. "Nonsense!" She began rooting around in her bag of potions. "Oh, and I *adore* your magical goggles, by the way," she added, glancing up at Benji.

His face turned shrimp pink. "Oh—um—thanks."

"They're not for trading!" I said quickly.

Ursula frowned. "I didn't say I wanted them."

I bit my lip. *Stop being so quick to judge. Maybe Ursula was just being kind.*

"Hey, Bloom!" A tiny, violet-haired figure waved to me from the beach.

"Oh, hi, Periwinkle."

She fluttered her sea sprite wings and flew over. "Your dad said you were coming to help." She hovered above the water, smiling. "Come and meet everyone."

Enchanted Splash Time was already underway. Groups of tiny campers were dotted around the lagoon. Some were gliding slowly on the backs of sea turtles. Others were brushing the golden flamingos' feathers. Some were building sand shapes on the beach that magically came to life.

"Wow, look at the shimmering shells on the turtles! Ooh and check out that sandcastle!" Benji hopped from one foot to the other. "It's got real people living in it!"

Periwinkle's eyes twinkled. "Oh yes, enchanted sand shaping is always popular. Last week we had a camper who made a dragon the size of a ship. It was rather naughty but so useful when we had to light the barbecue." She giggled, and her laughter sounded like tinkling bells. "Now, let me give you all a different group to work with. . . . Benji, since you like the sand makers, would you want to help them?"

His eyes lit up. "Oh yes, please!"

"And Bloom, why don't you join the kids on Quack Pack Time. It's a spotting activity," she added to Benji and Ursula. "The campers have to find a flock of yellow rubber duckies. They're great at hiding, so it's quite a challenge."

I smiled. The rubber duckies were some of the cutest magical creatures on the lake.

"And Ursula—" Periwinkle glanced across to where a few tiny campers were standing in the shallows looking a little nervous. "Maybe you could help with the beginner swimmers. We're just about to magic them some real water wings."

Ursula nodded. "Sure. I absolutely *love* teaching teeny-tiny helpless little ones to swim."

As I headed off to find the quack packers, I watched Ursula glide across to the young swimmers. *She really is confident in the water,* I thought. *Maybe she could even give me a few swim tips.* But then I glanced out to the deeper, darker lake beyond and shuddered.

I'll just stick to ducks!

7

"**WOW**, Marcie!" I smiled at the young camper who was pointing at the water. "It *is* a wish fish." The creature slipped past our legs, its scales shimmering in the sunlight. "Quick," I said. "Make a wish."

Marcie hesitated, closing her eyes in concentration. Then, in a flash, her hair turned purple.

I laughed. "Cool wish."

We waded across the cove, following the rest of our quack pack. "There's one!" I said, pointing to a tiny yellow bill poking out from a clump of seaweed.

"And another!" Marcie giggled at the yellow face peeking around a rock.

As I looked, my gaze drifted toward Ursula. She was in the shallows with three young campers. Their water wings flapped in the breeze. I

started to wave, when— *Huh?* I shielded my eyes
to see better. *Why is Ursula looking in her potions
bag?* I suddenly had a bad feeling in my belly,
and it had nothing to do with the cabbage candy
balls one of the little quack packers had tricked
me into eating.

"Um—excuse me, Pennywort..." I called to
the pond gnome counselor, who was leading our
activity. "I'm just going to check on something."

He nodded, and I splashed across the

sandbanks to Ursula's group. But before I could reach them, I saw a puff of pale orange smoke, and a strange smell of burnt seaweed filled the air.

"Stop!" I cried, running the last few steps. But it was too late. The campers had changed into tiny, furry sea otters, and zoomed past me. "What are you doing?" I asked Ursula.

"Helping them learn to swim," she said. "Like Periwinkle asked."

"But you're not allowed to do magical transformations on other people. It's in the camp rules." *Though I did turn one of my bunkmates into a Dalmatian once*, I thought guiltily, feeling my cheeks grow hot. *But that was an emergency!*

"Calm down, angelfish," Ursula said. "It's only temporary. If you'd seen how badly they were swimming before . . ." She shuddered. "But look at them now."

The little otters were rolling and diving and gliding under the water, chasing each other across the lagoon.

"Yeah, but—" I thought for a moment. Ursula *had* taught them to swim. Sort of. And now they were having loads of fun. *And it's not like I saw her take anything from them. . . .*

I was about to apologize for overreacting when I noticed she was playing with something in her hands. *Some sort of crystal ball?* As she moved it around, three shiny new bangles jingle-jangled on her wrist, too. *And hey—I'm sure I haven't seen that bow in her hair before....*

Just then, there was a POP noise and the three little otters changed back.

"Aw, I want to stay an otter," one of the little kids wailed.

"Me too!" her friend added.

The third camper was staring at Ursula. "Um—can I have my crystal ball back?"

"Sorry, no returns!" she crooned, stuffing the ball into her shell purse.

I frowned. "Hey there," I told the boy, who had started to cry. "Ursula will give it back. She's just teasing. Right, Ursula?"

The sea witch glanced over at Periwinkle, who appeared to be on her way over. "Catfish custard!" she muttered under her breath. But then she flashed us a shiny grin. "*Of course,* you *must* have it back," she said silkily. "Bloom's right, I was just 'squidding.'" She chuckled at her own joke. "Here—catch!" She tossed the crystal ball to the boy.

"And you two—" she called to the other swimmers. "Don't forget your bracelets and bow!" She glanced at me. "They asked me to take care of their things while they were swimming. Right, friends?"

But the little ones were too busy splashing around to reply.

"You know, Bloom," Ursula said, clasping her hands together and holding them to her chest, "the joy on people's faces is more than enough of a reward, don't you think? And now I must go. Ta-ta!"

"Was it something I said?" Periwinkle fluttered down next to me as Ursula dived away.

"Er—"

Before I could explain, the little boy camper held up his crystal ball to me. "Can you hold this while I swim, please?"

"Um—sure." I took the ball and watched him splash off into the shallows. *Maybe Ursula was telling the truth.*

"Oh, wow!" Periwinkle beamed as the boy dived into the water. "These guys are swimming so well. Ursula must be a very good teacher."

I frowned. *Yeah, she is.*

But did she try to make them pay a price?

8

"SO, let me get this right," Benji said as he added more sand to the giant lobster sculpture he was building with two little campers. "Ursula taught her group to swim by turning them into otters."

"Yeah," I said, "it was pretty cool, but—"

"And they really liked it?" he asked, patting the sand onto the lobster's pincer.

"Uh-huh. But Ursula took things from them—"

"For safekeeping, right? And then she gave them back, and Periwinkle was really pleased with what she'd taught everyone?"

I sighed. "When you say it like that, I feel bad for telling her off. But the little boy was really sad when she wouldn't return his crystal ball."

"Well, we all do silly things sometimes." Benji reached over to add extra sand to the lobster's eye. "Like yesterday when I turned your lunch into an owl."

"It flew off!" I laughed. "It's probably still fluttering around the Enchanted Forest somewhere."

Benji grinned. "Maybe we could go find Ursula. Ask her to do an activity with us. She's probably nice when you get to know her. Ooh, you know, snorkel stargazing starts soon. I'm sure she'd love that!"

I shuddered. *She would. But I wouldn't!* Snorkel stargazing was one of my biggest fears. It involved going underwater to view the magical starfish that glistened in Big Skies Bay. "Well, I'm actually not sure where Ursula went."

"Maybe she was embarrassed," Benji said, "about teasing the little kids. . . ."

"Do you think she went off to hide somewhere?"

Benji nodded. "When I feel bad about something, I hide under my bed. Like that time I decided to lend a hand mixing Mom's vegetable growing potion. My magical allergies made me sneeze, and the spell went everywhere. We had cauliflowers growing out of the kitchen floor for weeks!"

I chuckled. Benji could be quite clumsy. Then I realized what this meant. "But if Ursula is hiding in bed, she'd be in her cabin. And the water kids' cabins are *underwater*," I said.

I tried to imagine how I'd feel swimming in the deeper parts of the lake. I shuddered. *What if the kraken saw us? What if the ghost pirates rose up from their sunken ship? What if the grabby branched*

bramble bushes mistook me for a bubble ball and kept hold of me FOREVER!

"Hmmm...I'm sure I read about an underwater spell once." Benji frowned. "What was it called again...?" He scratched his head and hopped from one foot to the other. "Er—something like a babble-bonnet-breathing enchantment?"

"A bubble-head spell," I muttered. Jordy the merman had shown me it ages ago. It was one of the enchantments I'd memorized in case of emergencies. But I'd never used it before.

"That's it!" Benji's eyes sparkled. "It makes a bubble around your head so you can breathe underwater, right?"

"Yeah, but I've heard it doesn't last long," I replied.

"Then we'll have to be superquick!"

"You also need lots of magical items to make the spell work...like a piece of powerful sparkle silver cotton..." I put my hand behind my back in case he spotted the silver cotton in my enchanted friendship bracelet.

"Like this?" Benji held up his own bracelet, glinting in the sun, and I realized he'd twisted the same cotton through his.

"Oh, um—yeah . . . but you also need an enchanted waterbird feather."

Benji pulled something shiny from behind his ear. "I found this on the beach. I guess it comes from one of the golden flamingos."

I frowned. "B-b-but the spell doesn't work without a super-rare crystal from the very bottom of the lake, and there's no way you could have one of those."

Benji's eyes shone. He reached down to his swim trunks and flipped over the hem, and I saw a small green gemstone sewn into the lining.

"But how—"

Benji's goggles turned red. "My big cousin found it when she came here a few years ago. Mom insisted on sewing it into my shorts for extra water safety!"

I laughed, nervously. But my tummy felt like it had been turned into a spell-blender on superfast speed. Now that we had everything we needed for the enchantment, there was no excuse not to try it. *But what if the bubble-head spell doesn't work? What if it wears off when we're at the bottom of the lake?*

"Come on, Bloom, let's go check on Ursula. We'll be back in time for the rest of the Lake Whisper events today." Benji was already moving toward the water.

I followed reluctantly as Periwinkle waved us off, making us promise to come back for the barbecue beach party in a couple of hours' time.

"I've just thought of something," I said when we started wading deeper into the water. "We don't actually know which cabin Ursula is in." *And I definitely don't want to go ask Dad for the list. Then he'd know about our disagreement.*

"Maybe we can ask someone," Benji said. "There's bound to be loads of campers swimming around down there."

"I guess." I looked out across the lake and

shivered. *Am I really about to go underwater with all the weird magic and strange creatures floating around?* For a second I thought about racing back up the beach to rejoin the quack packers.

Nah, come on, Bloom, this is what Dad would do. He'd apologize to Ursula for misjudging her and make her feel welcome.

The water had begun to lap our shoulders. "We'd better do the bubble-head spell soon," I said, before I lost my nerve. I moved closer to Benji so his magical crystal would work for us both and I raised my (shaking!) hands—

"Water, water everywhere,

Bubble head, give us air."

Benji sneezed, but the sound was a little muffled, as my head was now encased in a large bubble.

Benji's bubble had appeared, too. He grinned at me and gave a thumbs-up, and we began to head underwater.

I held my breath, not fully trusting the spell.

"Whoa, it's like having your head stuck in a goldfish bowl." Benji laughed.

I tried to smile. But I couldn't shake off the worry that my bubble head would pop at any moment.

"This way!" Benji called, as we continued along the sand.... It was sloping steeply now, and after a few more steps, I noticed it felt harder, too. I glanced down and realized we'd reached the start of the sunken walkway that led to the cabins.

There's no going back now!

9

"**HEY**, guys!" Benji waved to a group of water-dwelling campers. "Do you know where Ursula's cabin is? She's a sea witch trainee."

"Hmmm . . . I think she's in Anchor, that way," one of the river elf kids called. "Across the bridge and turn left."

"Thanks!" Benji turned to me. "Whoa, it's really busy down here. You'd never know it above the lake."

He was right. It was bustling. And seeing so many campers and counselors out and about made me feel a little bit calmer about being underwater.

But then we came to the bridge.

I tried not to look down as we crossed over the deep ravine below. *What if there are water trolls underneath?* They were well-known for their naughty pranks. I stole a quick glance over the side of the bridge. No trolls. But it looked so dark and creepy!

What if I get lost, or caught in the weeds, or fall into a mind-mush marsh . . . ? I gripped the hand ropes tighter.

The trees were getting thicker and sea lamps glowed yellow, lighting the way along the path. I peered into the gloom, certain I could feel eyes watching us.

"Look out!" I tugged Benji down to avoid a shoal of electric swordfish buzzing over our heads. "They might pop our bubbles!"

"Oooooh! What was *that*?" Benji stumbled, and something slithered around his legs.

"Trip-you-up rope fish!" I cried as three more of the slippery critters darted out of the shadows. "Stand still until they pass—oh, and watch out for those volcanic anemones." I pointed out the patch of squatting creatures on the path just ahead of us. "If you accidentally squish one, it'll erupt with stinging lava juice. Come on, let's jog the rest of the way."

"Wow! I just love all the creatures down here," Benji panted as we passed a two-headed manatee and a phantom fish (*now you see it, now you don't!*). "We should sign up for the underwater night safari. I read about it on the flyer."

Luckily, we'd come to a crossroads, so I didn't need to answer.

We looked up at the signpost listing the names of the cabins. "There!" I said. "Anchor. It's pointing that way."

We followed the walkway through a maze of cabins, checking the name of each one as we passed. I reached up to tap my bubble. *Please don't pop yet!*

Anchor was the last cabin in the row. As we got closer, I felt my heart begin to thump faster. *What if Ursula doesn't want to see us? What if she unleashes a go-away spell that bursts our bubbles, and we get trapped down here with a whole school of trip-you-up rope fish?*

But as we stepped through the door . . .

"Empty?" Benji said.

I felt my shoulders relax. "That must be her bunk." The bed at the far end was surrounded by all sorts of trinkets. "They look like trophies!" I said, gazing at the Frisbees, crystal balls, wands, caps, jewelry, magic stones. . . . "I guess she got them from the campers she's helped. She said people like to give her gifts."

As I brushed past her nightstand, potion bottles tinkled against one another. Thankfully, none fell.

"Maybe we could leave her a note?" I suggested, looking around for parchment and a

water pen. "Tell her to come find us to do an activity together?"

"We could write it on this." Benji picked up a thick spell book poking out from under her pillow.

But as he lifted it, several loose pages fluttered out. I dived to grab them, and my eyes were drawn to a large doodle. *It looks like an idea board with a weird math equation*, I thought, scanning the page. . . . In big letters it read:

How to become the most powerful sea witch ever:

–make a wish for more wishes?

–steal an extrapowerful wand? (bonus: will look good on shelf)

–take someone else's magic as part of a trade?

More magic = more potions = more goodies for my collection = more power = more magic, etc.

Underneath there was a sketch of a giant Ursula with her arms full of treasure.

I gasped. This did not look like the drawing of someone who liked helping people for free. *She just wants to become the most powerful witch and get more stuff!* I shook my head. "So, she *was* doing deals with those little kids. I knew it!" And it seemed she was planning something even worse.

But Benji hadn't heard me. "What's that noise?" He cocked his head to one side. "Like something cracking open."

Huh? "That's what the bubble heads do when they're about to pop! Quick, we've got to get up to the surface." I stuffed the pages back inside the spell book and shoved it under the pillow before racing for the door.

As we whooshed back along the walkway, dodging two giant spell snakes and a large group of meowing catfish, I couldn't stop thinking about the page from Ursula's book. According to that drawing, Ursula wanted to be the most powerful magical being in the whole camp, and grab hold of everyone's most beloved treasures in the process. And it seemed she would do anything to achieve that goal.

We've got to stop her, I thought. But then I heard another crack in my bubble. I had more pressing problems.

"Quick, Benji!" I yelled. "We need to make like a rocket fish and zoom out of here!"

10

"**UM—THANKS**," I said, smiling at Jordy, the merman counselor who was holding out the snorkel mask to me. "But I might sit this one out."

We were back at the other end of the lake now—at Big Skies Bay, waiting in line for snorkel stargazing. But after our bubble heads had popped underwater, and we'd had to use the float-like-a-boat spell again to reach the surface, I was desperate for a break from lake activities.

"Are you sure? It looks so cool." Benji gestured to the stargazing sign next to the line. "See . . . it says the starfish have arranged themselves on the lake bed like the night sky constellations."

"I know, but—um—maybe I'll just wait for nightfall to see the actual constellations." I scratched around for an excuse. "And I'd better keep a lookout for Ursula."

I hadn't shared my worries about Ursula with Benji yet; first I wanted to be sure of my suspicions. And that meant talking to the sea witch herself.

"Okay." Benji checked that his goggles were on tightly. "I'll do a camera spell on my lenses so I can take some pictures for you!"

I smiled. "Awesome. And remember not to touch the starfish or they'll lose their sparkle." I grabbed one of the towels on a table nearby and trotted off toward the beach.

The shore was packed with campers doing various crafts. I dodged around, checking to see if Ursula was among the shell-spell jewelry makers, driftwood-wand builders, or campers decorating magical pebbles. But she was nowhere to be found. Eventually, I settled down by the lakeside to see if I could spot Benji snorkeling.

As I stared out into the bay, shielding my eyes from the sun and trying to work out which upside-down little blob in the water was him, a purple head suddenly popped out of the waves.

Ursula? I squinted to see what she was carrying. It looked like . . . a whole stack of pancakes? That couldn't be right. Then she moved, and the pancakes shimmered and wriggled in the sun. *Boiling barnacles! They're not pancakes. They're starfish!*

"Stop!" I yelled, scrambling to my feet. "You can't touch the starfish. They'll lose their sparkle!"

But Ursula had her back to me and didn't hear.

I looked around frantically, trying to figure out the quickest way to save the starfish. There was only one thing for it—a sound blast spell. I pointed my finger at her and said the words.

"Screeching monkey, growling bear,
Carry my words to that sea witch there:
PUT THE STARFISH BACK!"

A heartbeat later my shout spell hit Ursula—

She spun around in surprise, scattering the starfish back into the water. Then her eyes narrowed.

Uh-oh! She doesn't look happy.

11

"**WHAT'S** all the comm-ocean? Why were you yelling like a barnacled banshee?!" Ursula demanded as she met me in the shallows.

"Because no one is allowed to touch the starfish."

She frowned. "Really? Why not? There's loads down there. And I need their magic for my potions."

I felt a shiver of crankiness. So that's what she's up to—trying to make herself even more powerful by taking the starfish! "You can't just mix them up in your cauldron. They're living creatures."

Ursula cocked her head. "But how can I *help* people if I have no magical ingredients?"

"You don't seem to be doing spells to help. You're trying to get *more*—more magic and more trinkets!"

Ursula made a shocked face. "Angelfish! How can you say such a thing?"

I was about to tell her about the picture I'd seen in her bunk when a sudden breeze made my hair fly. I glanced up and a strange cloud drifted toward us.

"What is it?" Ursula asked, looking relieved at the distraction.

"It's a message cloud," I muttered. The counselors use them to communicate across the lake with one another. I peered up at it, reading the

words written on the side. *Don't forget the Sparkle Lagoon BBQ starts soon! Ask Ursula to join in, too!*

"Oh, how lovely," Ursula purred. "It must be from Periwinkle. The writing is the same color as her hair." She chuckled. "Well, we'd better swim. It's nearly dinnertime. And I have to admit, I get hangry without consistent snacks."

"Just a moment. First we have to find . . . Hey, Benji?" I shouted out to the lake.

One of the floating blobs closest to the shore upended, then waved. "Hi, Bloom! I'm nearly done!"

"Okay! We should—" I turned back to Ursula but— *Huh?*

Where did she go?

"So first I spotted Orion's belt. And then the Big Dipper . . ."

We were walking back to Sparkle Lagoon around the edge of the lake, and so far, Benji hadn't paused long enough for me to tell him about Ursula and the starfish.

"And then Jordy showed me Taurus, the bull constellation," he went on, nearly slipping on the sticky trail from a giant lake snail crossing in front of us. "It was so awesome. I think the starfish shimmered brighter than real stars."

No thanks to Ursula, I thought.

It was hard to focus on what Benji was saying because I couldn't stop thinking about her, and what she might be up to now. But as we rounded the path leading to Sparkle Lagoon, Benji let out a shout—

"Look, there's Ursula!" He waved to the sea witch, who was sitting in the shallows, helping prepare the food for the krill grill.

She glanced up and grinned. "*Whale-come* to the barbecue!" she called. "I'm cooking up a *fin-tastic* feast for the tiddlers." She gestured to the younger campers milling around. "Come join!"

"We're on our way—" Benji beamed at her.

"Ooh, I can't wait to tell her about the starfish. She'd love them!"

Yeah, a little too much! "Um—Benji, we really need to talk—"

"Whoa!" Benji pointed to a glistening lobster scuttling past. "Is that a Gilded Claw? I've never seen one before."

"Yeah, but Benji, I need to tell you something about Ursula—"

"Sure, Bloom—only we'd better go help, she looks so busy."

I followed him over to the table where Ursula was sitting. She was breaking up chunks of enchanted chocolate. "Guaranteed to give you sweet dreams," she giggled as she snapped another bar.

"Can I help?" Benji grabbed a bag of marshmallow cloud puffs. "Shall I pour them into this bowl?"

"Sure," Ursula said. "I *adore* a helping tentacle! But make sure they don't—"

Too late! A handful floated off.

"Oh, angelfish," Ursula purred. "That's the trouble with marshmallow clouds. You've got to keep a tight hold of them."

Not like starfish, I thought.

Ursula reached for a tray. "Periwinkle wants all the sea'mores ingredients put on here—oh, and Bloom . . ." She leaned in closer to me. "Sorry about our little *misunderstanding* earlier. I really should have checked about the starfish first."

Huh? Had she really just made a mistake? But that still didn't explain the drawing in her bunk.

"Benji, you find the tickle-toffee sauce," Ursula

said. "And Bloom, can you be a dear and get the crackling crackers and the seaweed sprinkles?"

"Oh, look! A seashell band is setting up." Benji bobbed up to get a better look. "I wish I could play an instrument. My mom bought me a set of magic pipes for my birthday, but the only thing I could charm was a big old hairy spider. It followed me around for days."

I chuckled. "That doesn't sound fun."

"Do you *really* wish you could play an instrument?" Ursula peered at Benji, her eyes sparkling. "I have a potion that could help with that. . . ."

My heart flipped, unsure what to do. But as she began to rummage in her bag, I saw my dad appear on the beach.

Benji spotted him, too. "Ooh, I wonder what's in that box Mr. Maj is carrying?"

"Hello, campers!" Dad called in his big, booming voice. "Come join me around the campfire. I have some exciting things to show you."

Ursula flipped the lid of her potions bag shut, frowning but following me and Benji as we joined the other campers already sitting in front of Dad.

He opened the box, and Ursula peered over the heads to get a better look. She smiled when she saw me watching.

"Exciting, isn't it," she said, giving me a toothy grin.

I nodded. But I couldn't shake off my overcoat of worry.

What would Ursula do next?

12

"**NOW**, as some of you might know, I am a collector of magical objects," Dad said, looking around at the campers. "I have a museum where I keep my favorite items. And inside this box are some of the strangest and most wonderful things I have found in Lake Whisper."

The campers glanced at each other, their eyes wide as dinner plates. I noticed Ursula's eyes were the biggest of all.

"Behold, an enchanted pirate doubloon."

The shine from the coin made me blink. Dad held it up, twisting it between his finger and thumb. It glistened and cast a golden ray across the sand.

"Towering toadstools!" Benji muttered. "That must have come from the ghost pirate ship that rises out of the lake each full moon."

"Legend has it, this coin can tell your fate," Dad said. "You just need to rub it against your chest and your future shall appear on the coin."

Ursula's hand shot up. "I want to try!"

Dad smiled patiently. "Knowing your fate isn't always such a good idea." He slid the coin back into the box and reached for another object.

"That's not very special." Ursula peered at the long green knobbly plant Dad pulled out. "Dried up old seaweed? Urgh!"

"Wait, is that—" Benji peered at it through his lenses. "A Rain Rag?"

Dad nodded.

"Oh, wow!" Benji's goggles fogged up with excitement. "It's a kind of weather weed. If you squeeze it, you can make it rain."

"Go ahead." Dad held it out to him.

Benji weaved his way past the other campers and took the plant from Dad, twisting it tightly. There was a loud *CRACK!* Benji sneezed, and then—

"It's raining!" one of the campers squealed as little droplets fell onto her face.

Dad chuckled, and his deep former-evil-sorcerer laugh made the ground shake violently, startling some of the tinier campers. "Good work, Benji! And now for another treasure..."

Each item Dad revealed was more exciting than the last. A solid silver feather from the Three-Headed Silt-Hopper, an aquatic bird that lived in the lake. A bright red pebble that could explode into a firecracker if you threw it into the sky. A shiny scale from the Healing Fish.

Dad said if you rubbed it on a wound, it would instantly make it better.

"Now this one might look small, but it has strong magic." Dad winked at me as he rummaged in the box. And then I saw why.

"The magical conch!" I breathed, as he held up the tiny pink shell he'd once shown me at the Museum of Mythical Objects. I shivered, remembering why the shell was so powerful.

"If you blow into the conch, you can summon a kraken!" Dad told the group.

"Flapping bats!" Benji muttered. "I'd *love* to see a kraken."

"Well, our kraken lives at the very deepest part of the lake . . ." Dad began.

"And only underwater creatures who are exceptional swimmers can make it that far," I added.

"Um, Mr. Maj . . ." A little pond gnome camper put his hand up. "What's a kraken?"

Before Dad could reply, Benji answered. "It's a type of sea monster," he said. "Oh—wait—I've got an Awesome Creature Trading Card about them. . . ." He began patting his pocket.

"Um—Benji," I whispered. "You're wearing swim trunks."

"Oh yeah." He blushed, and his goggle frames turned red to match. "I guess I'll have to show you later. But from what I can remember, they're enormous creatures with giant jaws, and long, sticky tentacles that can squeeze really tight and—"

"There aren't any krakens in the lake," Ursula interrupted. "I would have seen them."

"There is one," I said. "It's very fierce."

There were a few squeals from the littler campers. One small boy started to snuffle.

"It's all right," Dad said soothingly. "The kraken sleeps in a cave. And it will not wake unless someone steals its magical pearl."

"What pearl?" Ursula demanded.

"Well, the kraken is said to guard a special pearl that contains very powerful magic." Dad shrugged. "But no one knows for sure. The story of the pearl could just be a legend. And now for my next treasure—"

"How big is the pearl?" Ursula interrupted. "Where does the kraken keep it? Why is it so powerful? What can it do? How can I go see it?"

Dad smiled. "I'm sorry, I'm afraid I don't know, Ursula. No one has ever actually seen the pearl. If there even is one! Now let me show you something that is very real—not to mention very exciting. . . ."

Ursula scowled and folded her arms. But then her expression changed and became a little more thoughtful.

I shivered.

13

"A shell to summon a kraken? Can you believe it?" Benji hopped excitedly. We were helping gather up the empty plates and cups, while the campers danced to the seashell band. "I wonder how big the kraken is?"

"I'm happy not knowing." I put another plate on the tray I was carrying. "Can you pass me that cup? Dad taught me this amazing washing-up spell; it gets everything done so fast. I'll show you."

But Benji was gazing toward the shoreline. "Hey, there's Ursula. I think she wants me to join her."

I glanced over, spotting the sea witch in the watery shallows. But as soon as she saw me, she stopped waving and looked the other way.

Huh? That's odd. Maybe she thinks I'm going to tell her off again.

We'd been so busy clearing up after the bar-becue, I still hadn't had a chance to tell Benji what had happened with the starfish. Or the Ursula-shaped worry that was still sunk in my belly.

"I'll go check on her," Benji said, handing me another plate and cup. "Back soon."

"Wait!" I called. "There's something I need to—"

But just then, Marcie, the purple-haired camper from the rubber duckie search, appeared by my side. "Bloom, I've lost my bracelet," she sniffled. "The one I made at shell-spell class. Can you help me find it?"

"Sure—where did you last see it?"

"I don't remember."

I smiled. Here was at least one mystery I could solve. "Well, don't worry. My dad taught me a spell that can help find lost things. Want me to show you?"

She nodded.

"Okay, stand on one leg like this. Yep, that's it. Try not to wobble. Then say the magic words. . . .

*Look up, look down, look all around
Marcie's bracelet will now be found!"*

Marcie squealed. "It worked!" She held up her wrist and gave the shells on the bracelet a jangle.

"Awesome!" Over her head I could see Benji and Ursula deep in a chat. Benji's face looked serious. *What's going on down there?*

"Um—I'd better be going. So glad you found it, Marcie!" Then I padded down the beach to join them.

As I got closer, I noticed Benji was reading something—a long sheet of paper with lots of writing on it. But then a big bird swooped low over his head.

"Oh, wow!" he cried, peering up at it. "A rainbow gull!"

"Focus!" Ursula snapped, tapping the paper with a pen. "Now sign there!"

Benji glanced back at the sheet. "Oh yeah, sorry." He took the pen and began writing.

"And here's your potion," Ursula added, swapping the paper for a tiny green bottle. "Drink it up fast before the magic wears out!"

Magic? I ran the last few steps to reach them. "Benji! What are you doing?"

He swallowed the last of the potion down and sneezed. "Oh, hey, Bloom," he said. "The most amazing thing just happened—ACHOO!" He again sneezed so loudly his hair moved. "Oh, sorry," he muttered to Ursula, "magical allergies!" He blinked behind his goggles, then looked at me again. "Guess what? Ursula has made my dreams come true."

"She has?" I looked at the sea witch, who was busy stuffing the paper into her purse.

Benji grinned. "Yeah, Ursula just gave me this potion to turn me into a fish." He held up the little green bottle. "Now I can go all the way down to the bottom of the lake to see the kraken."

"What?" I froze. "You can't do that. It's too dangerous."

"Not if I'm an itty-bitty fishy. Ursula says the kraken wouldn't notice me. And anyway, I'm only going down to look. I won't wake it up—oh, wow, check out my hands. . . ."

Tiny scales had begun to pop out of his skin. His face looked a bit fishier, too. Sort of green and shiny with a pouty mouth. *And are those gills growing on the side of his head?*

"This is temporary, right?" I asked Ursula. "Like the sea otters."

She chuckled. "Of course. So long as Benji does me a favor in return."

Benji blinked fishy eyes at her. "What favor?"

"I want you to bring back the kraken's pearl. It'll be perfect for my collection. You see, I'm just like your dad, Bloom. I like collecting things, too. And that pearl sounds *extra* special."

"B-b-but I can't do that," Benji said. "If I do, I'll wake the kraken. And anyway, I would never take another creature's special thing."

"Suit yourself!" Ursula said.

"Don't worry, Benji," I said. "The spell will wear off. You can just splash around for a while until it does."

"Not so fast," Ursula said. "He made a deal. See—it's all here in black and white." She pulled out the paper I'd seen before and dangled it in front of me. "Read for yourself."

NO Takebacks

NO Tattling

X Benji

I scanned the page, my heart beginning to thump. I looked at Benji. "Did you sign this?"

He nodded, his big, fishy eyes wide and staring. "B-b-but I didn't see the bit about the pearl."

"You should always read the small print," Ursula said. "Especially in *o-fish-al* contracts!" She giggled at her own joke. Benji looked green—and it wasn't just the spell.

"B-b-but I got distracted. . . ."

"I saw!" I said, "by that rainbow gull. Come on, Ursula, you're not really going to hold Benji to this deal, right?"

"My tentacles are tied. It's a watertight, actual, real contract. If he doesn't bring me back that pearl, he'll stay a fish . . . FOREVER!"

14

BENJI shook his head. "I'd never steal anything." He turned toward the lake, his legs already changing into a tail. "Good-bye, Bloom," he called. "I'm sorry—"

Then he vanished into the lake with a loud *PLOP!*

For a moment I couldn't move. Had I really just seen my best buddy for the last time? I spun around to Ursula. "You won't get away with this! When I tell my dad he'll turn Benji back right away. He's the most magical person I know and—"

"Oh, do stop carping!" Ursula interrupted. She shoved the contract in front of my nose. "Read the small print again, Bloom: 'NO Takebacks. No TATTLING!' If you tell anyone, Benji will be in breach of contract, and he'll stay a fish forever." She chuckled. "*Cod* this be any clearer? Ha! Benji will just have to bring me the pearl."

"But he won't!" *Because he's kind and caring and would never do anything to hurt another living creature.*

Ursula snorted. "I'm sure he'll change his mind when a bigger fish starts sniffing around looking for supper."

Huh? My heart was almost thumping through my chest now. *What if something really did eat Benji?* I knew there were sharks and whales and loads of huge sea creatures in the lake. Not to mention the kraken!

Ursula rolled up the contract, and put it back in her shell purse. "So long, angelfish, I'm off to wait for my pearl." With that, she dived into the water and disappeared.

I stood there for a few minutes, looking out into the lake, hoping to see Benji pop up. But the water was pretty still—just the *slip-slop* sound of waves lapping against the shore.

Quick, Bloom, think! I racked my brain for a spell to turn Benji back, but even Dad had said how powerful a witch Ursula was. My spells were no match for hers.

I began to walk across the sand, hoping an idea would pop into my head. And then—like a freezing blast from a super-frosty snow spell—it did! I'll *take the pearl!* Ursula's contract didn't say anything about it having to be Benji.

But could I really swim to the bottom of the lake and face a ferocious sea monster? I felt my shoulders tense up. *No way!* I laughed—it was such a wild thought. Then another voice piped up. *If you don't, you'll never see Benji again.*

Urgh! I groaned. I walked faster across the beach. *If I do find the courage to take the pearl, I'll be stealing!* I stopped pacing and hugged my arms around myself, picturing how disappointed Dad would be to know his only daughter was a thief!

Though maybe I won't actually be stealing. Just borrowing. *As soon as Benji's transformed back, I could return the pearl to the kraken.* I just need to explain it all to the sea monster. *Wait—can a kraken even understand human words? And if it doesn't...*

I shuddered. *Come on, Bloom, you just need a plan.* I thought back to the days when Dad was planning the summer camp—lots of floating blackboards following him around our home, with all his ideas drafted out on them. I didn't know the blackboard spell, so instead I grabbed a piece of driftwood and began to scribble in the sand:

1. How do you swim to the bottom of the lake?
2. How do you take the pearl without getting eaten by the kraken?
3. How do you stop the rest of the campers from getting eaten by the probably now extra-cranky, woken-up kraken?

Just then, a tiny dragon-crab scuttled past, its fiery shell glowing brightly. . . . I stared at its shell for a few seconds, my mind ticking, then— *the conch shell! Of course.* I knew how to solve the last question. If I borrowed the enchanted conch shell from Dad's box, I could use it to lead the kraken safely away from everyone.

I tossed the stick away and raced back up the beach. I darted around various groups of campers until I spotted Dad standing on his head, levitating above the sand. I smiled sadly. Dad's flotation spell was legendary! I wished I could join in. Instead, I looked for the box.

"There!" It was a few feet away, tucked under a chair.

Head down, my tummy wobbling, I slipped past the group and crouched down next to the box. I did a quick check to make sure no one was watching, then reached inside.... For a second, I hesitated. *Should I go ask Dad first? But if I do, he'll find out about Benji, and then Benji will stay a fish forever!* I felt for the shell, then crept away.

Back on the shoreline, I threaded the conch onto my enchanted friendship bracelet.

I'm coming, buddy!

Now I just had to figure out the toughest bit of the plan: How to swim to the deepest part of the lake!

15

"**OKAY,** so a bubble-head spell wouldn't last long enough," I told myself as I looked out across the lake. "And besides, I don't have a magical crystal. And I can't use a transformation spell. Underwater animals are WAY too complicated." *Plus, I'll need human hands to take the pearl and a mouth to blow the shell to lead the kraken away from camp....*

For a second I contemplated asking Ursula for a potion. *But she's as reliable as a hungry cobra!* I'd probably end up stuck as a fish just like Benji.

I slumped down on the sand, and propped up my head with my hands. *Benji's going to stay a fish forever!*

"A fish, a fish," the lake seemed to say as it lapped against the shoreline. Then I saw it. A flash of lavender in the water. I scrambled to my feet and dived into the shallows. *Did I just see a wish fish?* I felt a surge of excitement. A wish fish could change me into an underwater creature! But first, I'd have to find it. I gazed around the lake, though there were so many brightly colored sea critters, shells, and seaweed, it was difficult to see much. . . .

If only Benji was here. He could use his magic glasses!

I crouched down to get a closer look, and my enchanted friendship bracelet dangled in the water. Wait—could my *bracelet* help me find the fish? Its magic alone wasn't very strong, but perhaps it could change my hands into something especially helpful!

I twisted the strands of the bracelet and spoke in a loud, clear voice. "Turn my hands into binoculars!" In a blink, I felt my palms tingle. Then my hands clenched into fists that stiffened and became lenses. "It worked!" I raised my new bin-oc-u-hands to my eyes and scanned the lake again. I looked left and right, then—

"There's one!"

The wish fish drifted past only a few feet away.

Now, Bloom! I told myself. *Make your wish! Turn yourself into an underwater creature.*

16

I felt an icy shiver. My bin-oc-u-hands vanished, and when I looked down—"I've got a tail!" I flopped down into the water, staring at my strange new body; the green scales were so shiny they made my eyes blink. *I really am a mermaid. Wow! I wish Benji could see this.*

Then I remembered about how he was a fish, and that I had a date with a kraken to steal its treasure, and my fins drooped. I gritted my teeth. *Come on, Bloom. You can do this!*

I headed out into the lagoon and glided around a few times, trying to get used to my tail. *It's more like wiggling than swimming,* I thought as I did a tumble turn and nearly bashed into a rock. *I need training wheels!* But there was no time to practice.

And so far, I hadn't even dared trying to put my head underwater. *What if my mermaid-breathing*

system doesn't work? I shuddered. *Okay, Bloom,
no more being a jelly-belly.* I crossed my fingers
and began: "Five . . . four . . . three . . . two . . . one-
and-a-half," I muttered. Then, when I could stall
no more—"ONE!" I dived and powered away to
find the pearl.

Down, down, down I swam. The farther I went,
the faster and smoother my swimming became.
It felt weird breathing underwater. *I just hope this
spell doesn't wear off.* I was a long way from the
surface now.

Dad had said the kraken's cave was at the
bottom of the lake, so I figured if I just headed
as deep as I could go, I'd find it. But as I swam
lower, and the lake became darker, the currents

began to spin my body left and right and round and round until I felt dizzy. My hair was longer now and I noticed it changing color—from green to red to flashing gold. That was the problem with the lake. Stuff happened that no one could explain.

Strange creatures kept appearing by my side, too. A shoal of chicken fish, clucking and strutting. A sea monkey swinging on a seaweed vine. And several tiny tyrannosaurus-sea-turtles, eyeing me curiously. *I hope they don't have any big brothers or sisters*, I thought, glancing into the shadows.

Suddenly, a woman with long yellow hair appeared in front of me.

"Ahhhhh!" I pulled back and crashed into a group of peanut-butter-and-jelly fish. I bounced off them back toward the woman. But then— *Oh, she's not real!* It was just a ship's masthead! My heart was thumping so loud, I was sure it would wake the kraken long before I could take its pearl.

I pushed through the sea branches to pass the woman and saw the rest of the ship she was attached to. *Wait a minute....* My eyes followed the long wooden sides of the hull, past portholes with cannons poking out of them and tattered masts fluttering in the current.

Surely this isn't the—? I gulped. *It is! The ghost pirate ship that rises every full moon.* I swam faster, feeling the gaze of a dozen phantom pirates on me.

And then something grabbed my tail.

17

"**HEY!** Let go!"

I spun around. "Benji?" I blinked at my buddy, who was tapping my tail with his fishy nose. His magical goggles glowed warm orange in the inky darkness.

He waggled his fins in a hello.

"Am I pleased to see you!" I hugged him tight. "Um—I'm guessing you're wondering what I'm doing here as a mermaid? Well, see, I've got this plan. *I'm* going to take the pearl for you!"

Fish-Benji's big eyes bulged.

"Don't worry, I'm only going to *borrow* it. Then when you turn back into yourself, I'll give it back to the kraken. Oh, and I brought this." I showed him the conch shell on my bracelet. "So I can lead the kraken away from the campers—hey, stop that!"

He was butting me with his head and gesturing back the way I'd come.

"I'm not leaving you as a fish forever," I said, sounding braver than I felt. "Come on, show me the way to the kraken's cave. I'm guessing you've been there already?"

Fish-Benji's body seemed to droop a little. Then he swam past me, his goggles lighting the way past the ship and deep into the darkest parts of the lake.

As we reached the lake bed, I strained to see, moving closer to Fish-Benji. "Thank goodness you've still got your goggles," I whispered. Not that I wanted to see *much*. Occasionally I caught a glimpse of a spooky critter lurking behind the rocks, and I quickly looked the other way.

Fish-Benji suddenly darted around a craggy section of boulders.

"Hey, wait for me!" I swam to catch up to the rocky bluff he'd found. "The cave is in here?"

Fish-Benji nodded.

"Okay, well—um—here goes nothing. . . ." I stretched out my hands and began to feel my way into the cave. I stopped, wondering if I had thought this through. My heart was pounding. My chest felt tight. My tail seemed to have turned to stone. "W-w-what if it eats me?"

Fish-Benji came close and we huddled for a moment. *Be brave, Bloom! I told myself. You can do this! For your friend!* I took a deep breath, moving again with Fish-Benji by my side.

For a few moments I couldn't see anything, then the cave opened out into a larger chamber. Nestled in a silver oyster shell on top of a huge rock was the pearl.

I blinked in its pretty glow. "It's as big as a golden goose egg! But—wait! Where's the kraken?" Fish-Benji and I glanced around the empty chamber. "Maybe the stories weren't true?"

The water seemed perfectly still and calm. There wasn't so much as a wave of magical kelp down here.

My shoulders relaxed. "Dad's going to be so surprised when I tell him there isn't a sea monster!" I swam across to the pearl and reached out to take it. But as soon as my fingers wrapped around its smooth surface, the ground beneath me wobbled slightly, followed by the other rocks on the cave floor.

Two giant yellow eyes popped open. I suddenly realized the rocks weren't actually rocks.

"Frosted fairies!" I cried. "I'm STANDING on the kraken!"

The whole chamber was filled with its knobbly bobbly body. Even the rock that the pearl sat upon was part of its back.

I grabbed the pearl and tumbled back toward the mouth of the cave with Fish-Benji. But the kraken's giant tentacles lashed out. "Hey!" I called. "Please don't hurt me. I'll give your pearl back as soon as I've broken a wicked spell. I promise."

The kraken let out a high-pitched howl in response.

"Quick!" I yelled to Fish-Benji. "Swim for your life!"

We shot out of the cave with the creature a

whisker behind us. Fish-Benji zoomed in front, guiding me through the rocks. But I could feel the kraken's hot breath on my back.

Fish-Benji darted left into a thorny thicket of sea trees, too tight for the kraken to follow. I squeezed in after him, and we weaved our way through the branches, deeper and deeper into the sunken forest.

"Well done! I think we lost it," I panted. But then—

"Helloooooo!" called a familiar drawling voice.

"Ursula?" I strained to see her through the thick foliage.

"Over here!" came the voice. "Behind the coral wall! It's a great place to hide from a nasty kraken."

As we swam around to find her, something thick and scratchy landed on top of us.

"Gotcha!"

"Ahh! Hey!" I gasped.

Ursula bobbed into view. "Hello, poor unfortunate friends. I thought there was something fishy when I saw you'd turned yourself into a mermaid." She frowned. "I guess you decided to take matters into your own tentacles, eh, Bloom? And did I just hear you were planning to give MY pearl *back to that monster...*?" She shook her head and sighed. "If there's one thing I can't stand, it's a double-crossing twister!"

I glared at her. "Well, it's better than being a mean-spirited trickster."

Ursula grinned. "Just give me the pearl and I'll let you go. If you don't, you'll be stuck down here. And then, when the sea monster starts looking for his evening snack . . ." She giggled.

I glanced at Fish-Benji, who goggled back with his big, wide eyes. "What can we do?" I whispered.

But all he could do was blow bubbles at me.

"Come on!" Ursula prodded. "Hand over that pearl!"

I was out of options. I looked down at the gleaming oval in my hands. We'd been bested. "Here, take it!" I shoved it through a gap in the net.

"Ooh, isn't it shiny and *so-fish-ticated*! Thanks, Bloom. And now I must leave."

"What? But you said you'd let us go!"

"Oh, yeah, that . . . Well—um—I changed my mind." Ursula turned to go. "Must fly! I have some potions to make. Bye-bye, angelfish!"

I felt a volcano of anger erupting in my belly. "I won't let her steal the kraken's pearl and leave us here."

Before I could change my mind, I put the conch shell to my lips and blew.

Okay, so maybe calling for the scariest sea monster in the world wasn't the best idea, but I'd promised I'd give the pearl back.

And if I couldn't do that, then I wanted to explain why.

18

I regretted my plan as soon as I heard the kraken's howl.

"Uh-oh!" I shrank deeper into the net, and Benji huddled close. "Um—maybe I could try a shield spell?" I whispered. But when I tried to think of the words, nothing seemed to make sense. "Urgh," I muttered. "Why does my magic go wonky in water?"

It was too late anyway. A large shadow darkened the water around us. The kraken suddenly loomed overhead, all angry eyes and waggly tentacles.

"P-p-please don't eat us!" I yelled. "I only took your pearl to release my friend here from a spell. See, a mean sea witch tricked him into becoming a fish, and I had to get the pearl to bring him home. I was going to return it to you, but then she took it. I'm so sorry."

The kraken's eyes bulged. It let out a horrible growl, and then it opened its giant jaws.

I screwed up my eyes and waited for the worst. . . .

Nothing happened.

"Huh?" I opened one eye and saw the creature's tentacle looming toward me. "Wah!" I gasped, shutting my eye again. But I suddenly felt the weight of the scratchy net vanish.

When I looked again, we were free.

"D-d-did you just save us?" I asked the creature. "That was so kind—hey!" I chuckled, as it prodded me with its tentacle. "That tickles!"

The kraken paused, cocking its giant head to one side as though it was waiting for something.

I glanced at Fish-Benji. "Um—what's going on here?" But then—

"Hoi!" I cried, as the kraken did it again. I moved back a little to see the creature more clearly. "This is what my dog does when he wants to play ball," I said to Fish-Benji. I really didn't want to play games with a sea monster the size of a school bus. But as it reached out again, I suddenly realized what it was doing. "Wait—is it the conch you're pointing to?" I held up the tiny shell. "You like the noise it makes?"

The kraken's eyes widened.

Okay, I hope I'm reading this right. . . . I lifted the shell to my mouth and blew.

The creature let out a long, low sigh, and the color of its face changed from fiery red to pale apple green. I blew again, and it started to purr.

I smiled. "All that fuss, and you're just a big old cuddly octo-puss!" I cleared my throat. "Um—kraken, I'm going to have to go now—no, no, it's okay. See, I have to find Ursula. She's the sea witch I told you about. I want to get your pearl back, just like I said. Is that all right?"

The kraken's tentacles tilted a little.

"Don't worry. I'll come back. I promise."

Huh? Had I just promised to return to the scariest place on the planet to visit a kraken? *Whoa.* I guess becoming a mermaid wasn't the only change I'd made today.

Was I starting to actually *like* the lake and its creatures?

I sped up my swimming, deciding to figure it all out later. We had a pearl to return!

WE headed straight for Ursula's cabin. Where else would a sea witch take a magical pearl, if not back to her potion kitchen?

As we rose up from the depths of the lake, the water became clearer. I kept glancing at Fish-Benji. *Hmmm...that's weird.* The contract said he'd change back when Ursula got her pearl. What if she had tricked us again?

But there was no time to worry. "There it is!" I said, spotting Ursula's cabin. "Come on, let's go take a look."

We swam past the door and hovered underneath the window. Then we bobbed up and peeped inside.

"Wow!" I breathed. "So much smoke!"

Ursula was standing in the center of the room, where she'd set up a tiny cauldron by her bed. Underneath it a strange purple flame

roared. Colorful smoke rings were rising from the top of the potion as she added more and more ingredients.

I frowned. *Fires and cauldrons? Didn't Ursula follow ANY camp rules?* Neither were permitted in the cabins.

Then I saw her reach for the pearl. . . .

"Quick!" I called to Fish-Benji as I zoomed for the door. "We've got to stop her." I yanked open the handle and burst inside. "Put that pearl down!"

Ursula froze before an icy smile appeared on her face. "Do you really think one little mermaid and an itty-bitty useless fishy can tell a sea witch what to do?"

"B-b-but I'm not a fishy!" said a warbling voice. "Not anymore!"

Huh? "Benji?" I glanced behind me. "You can speak again!"

His scales were popping like bubbles. His pouty mouth was shrinking, and his tail had already changed back into two legs.

Ursula chuckled. "I think someone's forgotten that humans can't breathe underwater."

Benji's cheeks were puffed up as he tried to hold his breath; he looked like he'd burst at any moment.

"Go!" I said. "Use the float-like-a-boat spell and get back to the surface."

Benji looked at Ursula, then me, and gave an apologetic frown. He swam out of the door and vanished.

"Oh, cry me a river!" Ursula said in a mock-sad voice. "The poor mermaid has been left all alone."

"I'm perfectly fine!" I said, hiding my shaky hands behind my back. "I want you to return the pearl to the kraken."

Ursula's eyes narrowed. "No."

I swallowed a few times. "Okay, then, if you won't give it back," I said, trying to steady my voice. "Then I'll have to—um—*take* it back!"

Ursula laughed. "And just how would you do that?"

"Um—with a lost-property retrieval spell!" I blurted out, suddenly remembering the enchantment I'd shown little Marcie earlier. Okay, so I didn't have one leg to stand on, but I hoped a tail would work just as well.

"Look up, look down, look all around,
Kraken's pearl will now be found!"

"Blocked!" Ursula said, raising her hand. "Really, Bloom? Did you actually think that a baby's charm would defeat a powerful witch like me? Let me show you some real magic. . . ."

She grabbed a red potion off her table and

threw the contents up into the water. A giant cloud of spiky sea urchins cascaded down, thundering across the cabin floor like bristly bowling balls.

"Whaaa!" I yelled, scrambling for the door.

But just then someone pushed past me, their hands raised.

"Stones and iron, strong hard shells. Create a shield and deflect all spells!"

ACHOO!

"Benji!" I gasped. "You're back!"

The spiky sea urchins bounced off the shield spell that he'd just made.

He grinned at me through his bubble head. "Couldn't leave you to take on a sea witch by yourself! Oh—watch it!"

Ursula popped the shield with a giant pin. "Take that, you annoying shrimps!" And she blasted us with ink from her tentacles.

"Not so fast!" I leaped up and did a backflip, swatting the wave of ink away with my mermaid tail.

"Slam dunk!" Benji cried, as it splattered into the cabin wall. "Awesome move, Bloom."

Ursula let out a growl. "Well, I've got some moves of my own." And she grabbed another potion bottle and began to shake it like soda. Then—

POP!

Benji sneezed as the lid flew off and dozens of green eels exploded out of the neck of the bottle. They grew longer and larger as they hurtled toward us.

"Look out!" I yelled, as the eels wrapped

themselves around Benji's arms and legs. But in a blink they were around me, too, squeezing and pressing and squishing and tying me up in knots.

"Trapped!" Ursula said. "Like sardines in a can. And now I can get back to my potion—" She turned and reached for the pearl again. "Once I add this little beauty into the mixture, I'll be able to make the most powerful spells in the world! Then think of the treasures I'll be able to take from the campers—*mwahahahahaha!*"

Do something, Bloom! I thought desperately. *You have to protect the camp. Besides, you promised the kraken!*

20

OF course! The kraken! I glanced at the shell on my enchanted friendship bracelet, then wriggled my wrist free. I brought the conch up to my lips and blew.

Ursula looked up. "What in the name of Neptune—?" Then she saw what I was doing. "Stop that!" She raced across the room and ripped the shell from my bracelet, tossing it away.

"Where was I . . . ?" Ursula went back to her cauldron and reached for the pearl. She held it above the bubbling contents, whispering spells under her breath. "And now, angelfish," she said, smirking at us, "watch and learn as I become the most powerful sea witch in the world!"

But just as she dropped the pearl, a long tentacle shot through the window and caught it before it landed in the cauldron. The kraken let out a thundering growl.

"Hey!" Ursula yelped. "Give that back!"

But the kraken ignored her. Another one of its wiggly arms shot through the door, this time reaching toward us and flicking off the eels.

"Great work!" I shouted, wriggling free. "Thanks, kraken!"

Ursula let out a shriek. "I won't let you take the pearl!" She grabbed a potion from her table and flipped off the lid. She threw a gray liquid toward the kraken's tentacles.

"ACHOO!" Benji sneezed, and his eyes boggled behind his goggles. "Uh-oh, that looks a lot like a turn-to-stone potion! My mom used one to build our garden wall."

"Oh no!" I cried. "Look out!"

But just as the liquid reached the kraken, the creature twisted the pearl toward it, and the potion stopped in midair. It turned into a solid rock and fell to the floor with a giant *CRASH*. The thud made all Ursula's potion bottles wobble, then topple, then—

SMASH!

"Whoa! Look at the mess!" Benji gasped, as the contents from the broken spell bottles mixed into one another, making a giant multicolored floating cloud. "That pearl really *is* powerful."

Ursula gave a howl of anger. "NOOOOOO!" Her tentacles moved around wildly, as she tried to separate the potions.

"Come on," I whispered to Benji. "Let's go thank the kraken properly."

The creature's eyes lit up as soon as it saw us swim out of the cabin.

"Hey!" I chuckled as it grasped us up in its

tentacles and hugged us close. "Um—thanks for coming to the rescue."

After a quick squeeze, it let us go and waved good-bye. Then it drifted off into the depths of the lake, still clutching its pearl.

"I guess we'd better go talk to Ursula," I said.

We poked our heads back in the bunkhouse, and she shot us a glare.

"I hate this camp," she hissed. "And I hate all this junk! It's useless compared to that pearl." She gathered all her scattered trinkets and

127

tossed them out the window. "But most of all," she said, glaring at me, "I HATE MERMAIDS!"

"Um—I think we should be going," I whispered to Benji.

As we turned to leave, I noticed something small and pink lying on the floor. "The conch!" I picked it up and followed Benji outside.

The door slammed loudly behind us.

"Hey, look!" Benji pointed to the cloud of Ursula's collection of trinkets floating around in the water. He reached up and caught a cap and a Frisbee before they could drift away. "Maybe we could take these things back to camp?"

"Great plan!" I caught the little shell box, the one I'd seen the swamp fairy trade with Ursula. "There's a T-shirt floating there," I said. "We could wrap some of the things up inside."

"And I'll fill this cap, too. . . . Oh, and I think we'd better be heading back soon," Benji said, looking at my tail, which had begun to grow feet at the end. "Your wish is starting to wear off!"

21

BY the time we reached the surface, I was back to myself.

"Will you miss being a mermaid?" Benji asked as we waded through the shallows of the lagoon.

"Maybe a little," I said. "I was definitely a better swimmer. But I think I still prefer dry land."

"Oh, me too." Benji wriggled his toes in the sand, and his goggles glowed sunshine yellow.

I smiled. It was good to have my buddy back. I'd missed being able to talk to him. "At least you got to see the kraken."

Benji's face turned beetroot. "Er—true, but if I hadn't been so distracted by everything I wanted to see and do . . . maybe I'd have paid more attention to that contract."

"In some ways I'm glad you didn't," I said. "It forced me to face my fears. And now that I know how cool Lake Whisper actually is, I never want my worries to hold me back again. Like with the kraken. I thought it was the scariest monster ever, but it turned out to be kind and sweet."

Just then I heard a voice calling my name. I glanced up.

"Dad?"

He was standing on the sand at the top of the beach, waiting for us.

"Uh-oh!" I looked at all the trinkets we were carrying. "How are we going to explain all of this?"

I wasn't sure Dad would approve of me swimming to the bottom of the lake to take the kraken's pearl.

Benji frowned. "Do you know any fast-acting disappearing spells?"

But it was too late.

"Ah, I see you've been doing a little lost-and-found tidying up," Dad said, walking down to meet us.

"Um—sort of," I said, not meeting his gaze.

"Well, that's very kind of you. I'm sure all the campers will be pleased to have their belongings back."

I forced myself to look at Dad's face and saw his eyes were twinkling.

"Perhaps I can help," he added. "If you could lay all the items on the sand . . . yes, that's right, spread them out."

"There's so much stuff," Benji said, as we placed it in rows. "Wands, charm bracelets, shell necklaces . . ."

"A lot of shell necklaces!" I said.

"And now if you'd just step back a little." Dad passed his hand over the top of the objects and whispered a few words under his breath. Benji sneezed and the items began to fade. In seconds they were gone.

Benji's eyes were the size of giant clams. "How did you do that?"

"Just a little returning spell. And now the items will be safely back with their owners."

I smiled, but inside my heart was thumping. There was one item I still had to return. "Um— Dad . . ." My throat suddenly felt full of sand. I swallowed a few times, then took a deep breath. "I'm so sorry but I had to borrow this." I held out the little conch shell. "I should have asked first, but—"

"No apology necessary." Dad smiled at me knowingly. He took the shell and held it in his palm for a moment, turning it one way and then the other. "Hmmm, isn't it interesting that such a tiny object that you might overlook in a tray of bigger, more colorful items can be so strong and powerful when it needs to be. It reminds me a little of you, Bloom. And you, too, Benji."

My buddy's glasses steamed up. "Oh—um, thanks."

"Sometimes all you need is the strength of a solid friendship to make you step up and believe in yourself. Wouldn't you both agree?"

We nodded.

Dad looked out to the lake where the sun was starting to go down. "We often underestimate ourselves. Others, too. Even the scariest creatures can be kinder than we imagine." Dad looked at me, then held out the conch shell. "What do you think, Bloom, shall we return this to the kraken?"

"Huh?" I blinked at him. "You mean you're not going to put it back in your museum?"

"No." Dad tipped the shell into my hand. "I

think it belongs with its rightful owner. Perhaps you could return it. And now, I must get back to the beach party. There are sea'mores left, if you're hungry."

Benji's tummy rumbled. "Yes, please!"

Dad turned to go, then stopped. "Oh, and I'm sorry to report your friend Ursula won't be joining us. I've just gotten a cloud message from one of the underwater counselors. I'm afraid she's requested to leave."

"Really?" I looked at Benji.

"Um, that's a shame," he mumbled.

"It is," Dad sighed. "But camp life isn't for everyone. Perhaps she'll come back next year."

"Maybe," I said, not quite meeting Dad's eyes.

With that, he bowed, then turned and walked away, his cape billowing in the breeze.

I looked back at the lake. "It's a beautiful sunset, Benji."

"Yeah," he said, squinting. "The sun looks just like a big, fiery pearl!"

"Mmm, I think I've had enough of pearls for one day."

Benji grinned. "How about we dry off and join the party?"

I nodded. "We're going to need to eat lots of snacks to keep up our energy."

"You mean for all the dancing we're going to do to the shell band?"

"Yeah, but we've also got to figure out an awesome magical submarine spell so we can go down and visit the kraken to return the conch. Because I don't know about you, but I thought he looked a little lonely down there."

"But not anymore!" Benji smiled. "Now he's got us!"

"Exactly!" I linked my arm through Benji's as we set off up the beach. "Who'd have thought I'd be the one wanting to go back underwater?"

Benji chuckled. "Well, I guess *any-fin* is possible when it comes to Lake Whisper. As you said, water magic really is mysterious and unpredictable!"